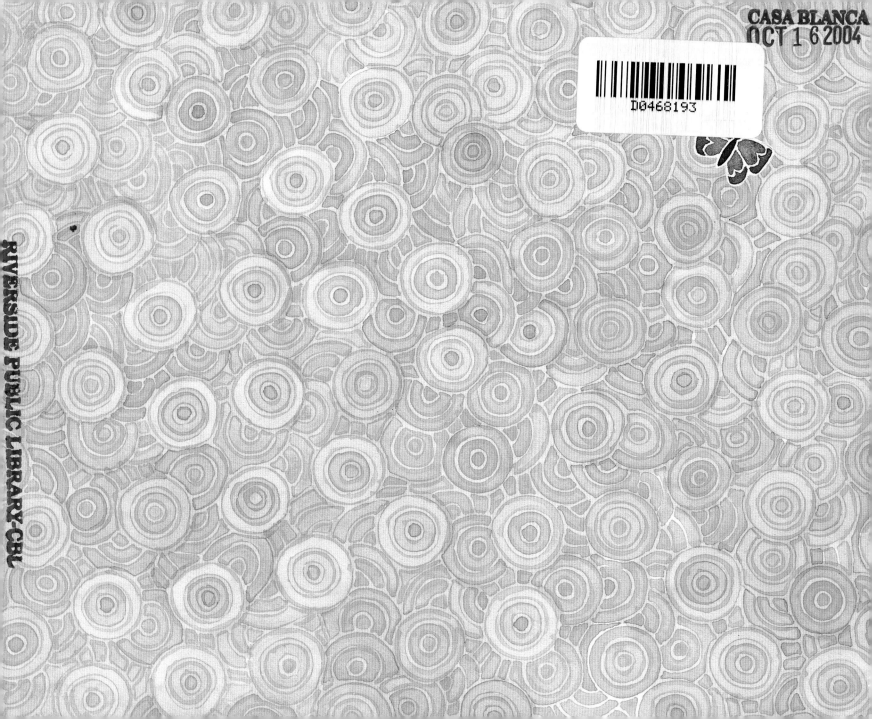

For my very special niece and nephews,

Ginny and JohnTaylor Schneider,

Timothy, Keith, and Philip Swistak. —J.M.

Book design by Lucy Nielsen. Typeset in Gill Sans and ITC Officina.

Printed in Hong Kong.

Library of Congress Cataloging-in-Publication Data

Mammano, Julie.

Rhinos who skateboard / by Julie Mammano.

p.   cm.

Summary: Skateboarding rhinos grind curbs, pop ollies, rip through
tunnels, and biff on bumps. Includes a glossary of skateboarding lingo.

ISBN 0-8118-2356-3

[1. Skateboarding-Fiction. 2. Rhinoceroses-Fiction.] I. Title.

PZ7.M3117Rd   1999

[E]-dc21   98-36201   CIP

AC

Distributed in Canada by Raincoast Books

8680 Cambie Street

Vancouver, B.C. V6P 6M9

10 9 8 7 6 5 4 3 2 1

Chronicle Books, 85 Second Street

San Francisco, California 94105

www.chroniclebooks.com/Kids

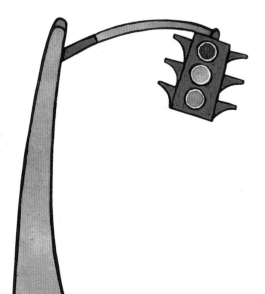

Rhinos Who Skateboard

JULIE MAMMANO

chronicle books · san francisco

Rhinos who skateboard can't wait to skate.

They jump on their boards and . . .

SPLIT.

They GRIND some curbs

then grab some GRUB and head for the park.

They RIP
through tunnels.

Rhinos who skateboard **TOSS SICK FLIP TRICKS.**

They hit STELLAR jumps.

So they KICK IT and plan their next urban MEGA SESH.

Wheel Chatter

bail to quit or try something else

biff to mess up

choke to mess up

cool really good

drag not really fun

dude the way to address someone *or* what you call someone

flip trick to stylishly flip the board

geekfest a gathering of nerds

grind a trick using the metal part between the wheels (called trucks)

grub food

kick it to relax

lame air a bad jump

mega really big

mellow relaxed

nab to get

ollie to jump up with the board sticking to the feet

pole jam a trick done off a pole

pop quick jump

posse a group or bunch

psyched excited

rail slide to slide down a rail

rip to skate really well

road rash scraped up skin

sesh session

sick great

slap the sound a skateboard makes when it lands

split to leave

stellar great

street biscuit a rock or hard chunk of crud

throw down to do a trick or jump

toss to do a jump or trick

totally very

vibe a feeling of atmosphere

way very

wicked really bad or really good

yahoo to be over confident, but not very good; a poser

Rhinos' heads are hard.
Kids' heads aren't.
Wear protective gear and...

SKATE SMART.

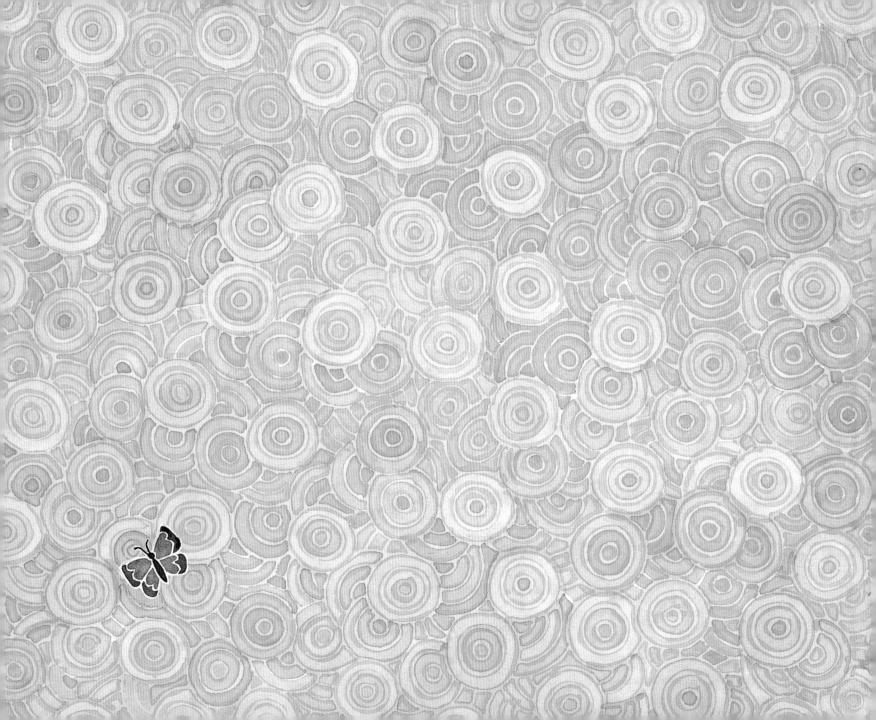